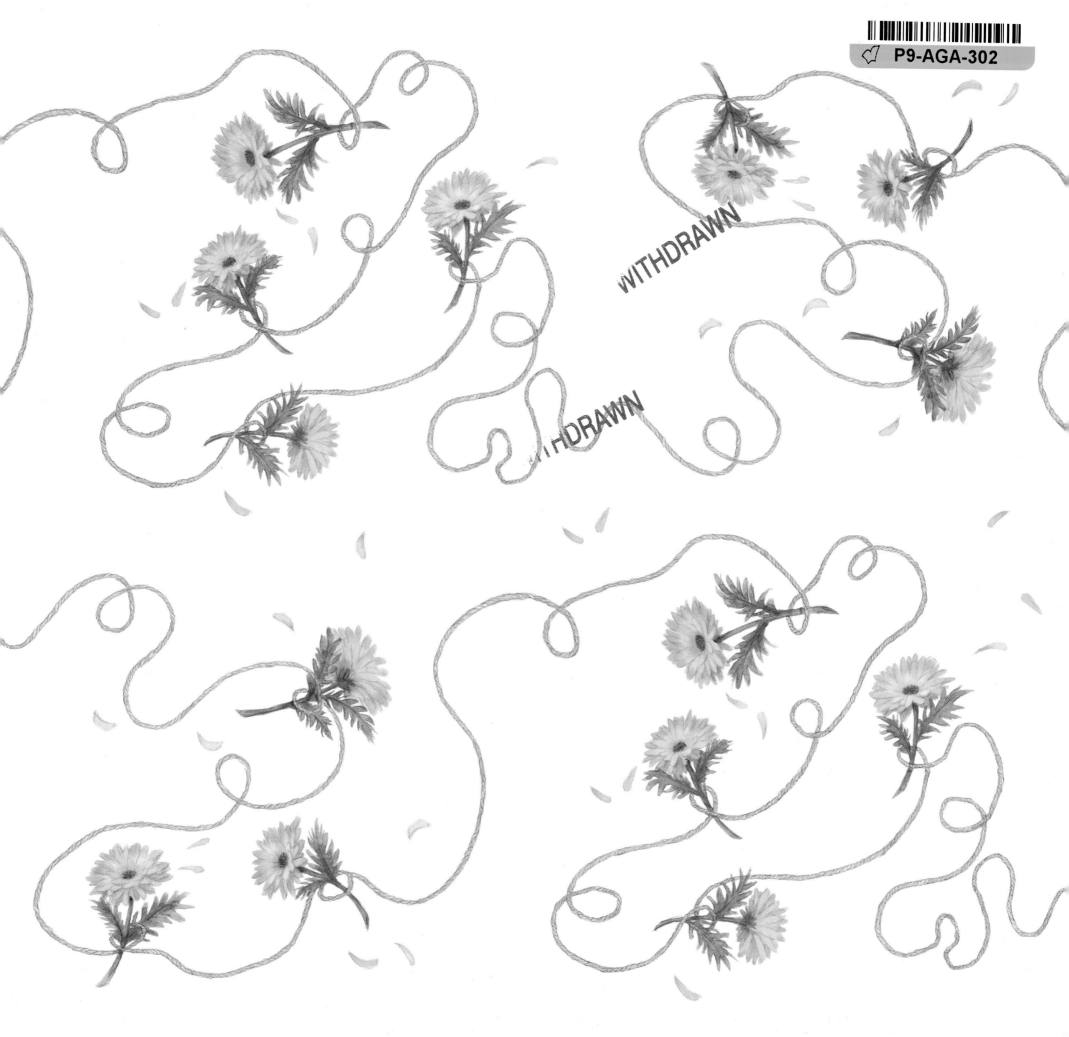

For my dear mum, who, when I was little,
knitted me a rainbow jumper, and first
inspired my love of wool. – D.C.

To my family and my niece Sungah,
and nephew Luah, who fully supported
and encouraged me with love. – S.L.

This book belongs to

_____

The artwork in this book is handcrafted using watercolour and
coloured pencils and finished with digital methods.

First published in 2020 by Floris Books. First published in the USA in 2021. Text © Dawn Casey 2020
Illustrations © Stila Lim 2020. Dawn Casey and Stila Lim have asserted their right under the Copyright,
Designs and Patent Act 1988 to be identified as the Author and Illustrator of this Work
All rights reserved. No part of this book may be reproduced without the
prior permission of Floris Books, Edinburgh www.florisbooks.co.uk
British Library CIP data available. ISBN 978-178250-658-4
Printed in Poland through Hussar

FSC
MIX
Paper from
responsible sources
FSC® C015559
www.fsc.org

Floris Books supports sustainable forest management
by printing this book on materials made from wood that
comes from responsible sources and reclaimed material

Spin a Scarf of Sunshine

Dawn Casey and Stila Lim

Floris Books

On a gentle slope in rolling hills stood a little house of wood and stone.
There were hens and bees and apple trees, bright flowers and soft green grass.
And Nari had a little lamb of her very own.

All year, Nari's little lamb ate the soft
green grass, and it grew big and strong.
Its fleece grew thick and warm.

Stroke – stroke

Winter turned to spring. Nari's little lamb grew into
a fine sheep, with soft white wool.
Papa cut the sheep's fleece.

Snip ~ snip

And Nari washed the wool clean.

Splash – splosh

Nari brushed the wool smooth.

Brush – brush

And spun it into yarn.

Drop – spin

In the summertime, the cottage garden was full of flowers.
Nari gathered armfuls of marigolds.

Skip – pick

She put the flowers in a big pot of water. It bubbled over the fire.
Mama dyed the yarn, yellow as summer sunshine.

Stir – stir

On autumn evenings, Nari sat by the fire, knitting.

Clickety-click
Clickety-click

Sometimes she made a mistake.

Clickety-click   Clickety-clonk

But she tried and tried again.

By wintertime, Nari had a fine new scarf.
Nari wore her scarf in mist and mizzle, storm and snow.
It kept her snug and warm.

Mmmm

Time passed. Nari grew tall. The scarf grew tatty.
One day, Nari said goodbye to her old scarf. She put it onto
the compost heap, with the carrot tops and apple cores.

Drop - flop

The sun shone and the rain fell on the compost heap.
By and by, the apple cores, the carrot tops and the old scarf
turned into compost, with a little help from the worms.

Wiggle - munch

Nari dug the compost into the earth,
and it made the earth good and rich.

Dig – dig

The rich earth helped the plants to grow.
The grass grew soft and green,
just right for a little lamb.

Baaaa

The Wool Cycle, from Sheep to Scarf

1 Nari's lamb ate lots of grass and grew big and strong. It became a sheep.

2 Papa sheared the sheep to keep it cool in summer.

3 He kept its warm fleece.

11 Nari dug the compost into the earth to help the plants grow.

10 Worms helped turn the scarf into compost.

4 Nari washed the fleece.

5 She brushed the wool smooth.

6 And she spun it into yarn.

7 Nari gathered bright flowers.

8 She helped Mama dye the yarn.

9 Nari knitted the yarn into a new scarf.

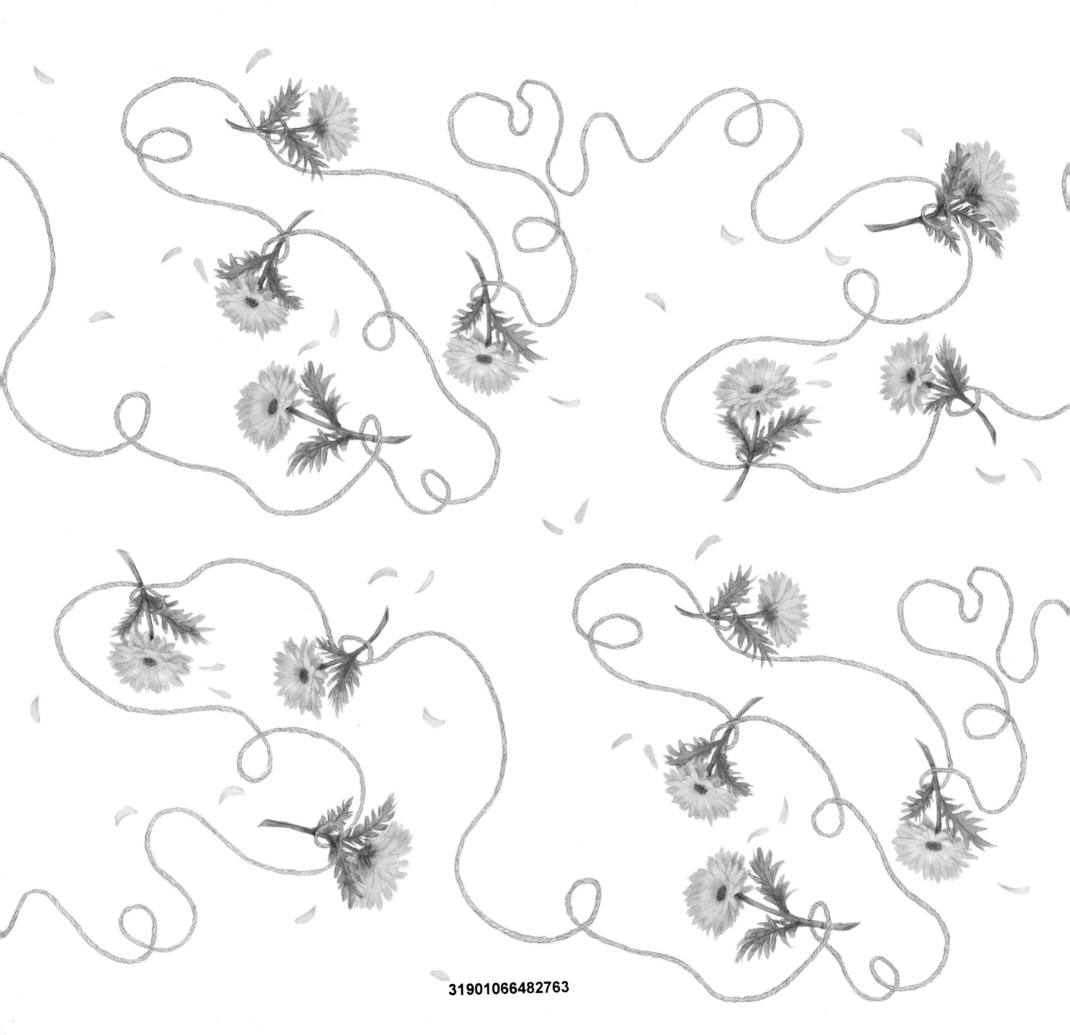

31901066482763